D0493329

Farmer George
and the New Piglet

Other books in the series:

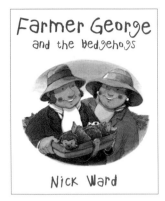

Farmer George and the Hedgehogs

Nick Ward

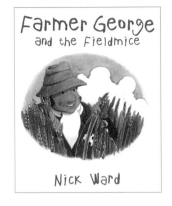

Farmer George and the Fieldmice

Nick Ward

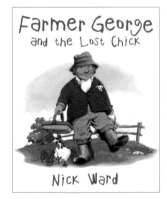

Farmer George and the Lost Chick

Nick Ward

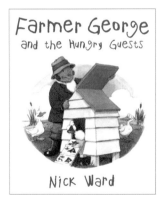

Farmer George and the Hungry Guests

Nick Ward

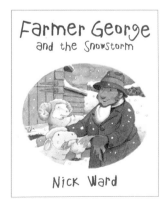

Farmer George and the Snowstorm

Nick Ward

Farmer George

and the New Piglet

NICK WARD

CHRYSALIS CHILDREN'S BOOKS

For Anna and William

**EAST SUSSEX
COUNTY LIBRARY SERVICE**

07-Aug-03	PETERS
956847	

A PAVILION CHILDREN'S BOOK

First published in 2001

This paperback edition first published in Great Britain in 2003 by
Chrysalis Children's Books
64 Brewery Road
London N7 9NT
www.chrysalisbooks.co.uk

Text © Nick Ward 2001
Illustrations © Nick Ward 2001
Design and layout © Pavilion Books Ltd

The moral right of the author and illustrator has been asserted

Designed by Ness Wood at Zoom Design
Cover design by Keren-Orr Greenfeld

All rights reserved. No part of this publication may be reproduced, stored in a retrieval system,
or transmitted, in any form or by any means, electronic, mechanical, photocopying, recording
or otherwise, without the prior permission of the copyright holder.

A CIP catalogue record for this book is available from the British Library

ISBN 1 84365 022 3

Set in Bell MT
Printed and bound in Singapore by Kyodo
Colour Origination in Hong Kong by AGP Repro (HK) Ltd

2 4 6 8 10 9 7 5 3 1

This book can be ordered direct from the publisher. Please contact the Marketing Department.
But try your bookshop first.

One day, Farmer George came home from market carrying an old cardboard box. "Not another hungry mouth to feed," sighed Dotty.

"Meet Perry," said Farmer George.
"He looked so miserable, I just had to
buy him."
"Oh George," smiled Dotty. "You
already work too hard."

Farmer George introduced Perry to Ronan, Prudence and their piglets. "Don't worry, they'll look after you," he said.

But as soon as George left, Perry scooted through a gap in the wall…

…and when Farmer George got back to his farmhouse, Perry the piglet was already there.

"How did he get here?" gasped Farmer George.

After tea, Farmer George
took Perry back
to the sty.

But Perry squeezed through the gap in
the wall, and by the time Farmer
George got back to the farmhouse…

…Perry was sitting in the farmer's favourite chair.
"Well I never!" said George. "He's done it again!"

"He may as well stay here tonight," said Dotty. So Perry curled up in the armchair.

But in the middle of the night, Perry got lonely. He wanted Farmer George. "Wee!" he cried. "Wee, wee!"
"Oh no, he's afraid of the dark!" moaned George.

Farmer George put on his
dressing-gown and sat up all night
reading stories to the baby pig.
In the morning he was very, very tired!

Everywhere Farmer George went, Perry went with him,

whether he was milking Hermione, feeding the ducks or brushing Billy!

And every night Perry had to have a story. Farmer George grew more and more tired. "What am I going to do?" he asked Dotty.

"Poor Perry will just have to get used to his pigsty," said Dotty. "Or he'll have to go back to market."

So Farmer George took Perry down to the sty one last time. "There's nothing to be scared of," he said, settling down in the straw.

"It's nice and…"
But Farmer George
was so tired he fell
fast asleep!

"Wee!" squealed Perry.
"Ssh!" whispered the other piglets.
"Farmer George is tired. Let's go out and play."

"No," squealed Perry.
"Oh, please!" they said.
"NO! NO! NO!"

Dotty was hanging out the washing
when she heard a
dreadful squealing.

"Oh dear," she cried.
"What's going on?"
And she rushed off to the pigsty…

…only to find Perry jumping and rolling in the mud with the other piglets.

"This is brilliant," Perry cried. "Let's do it again!"

"But where's Farmer George?" Dotty
wondered. She looked through the
window of the sty.

There was Farmer George, snoring
louder than Prudence and Ronan!
"Don't worry, George," said Dotty.
"I think Perry is perfectly happy now!"

And he was.

More titles available from Nick Ward

THE TADPOLE PRINCE
Everyone's heard of the Frog Prince, now meet the tadpole prince in this
fast-paced and hilarious twist on the traditional fairy tale.
Hardback ISBN 1 84365 016 9 £9.99

And from the Farmer George series

FARMER GEORGE AND THE SNOWSTORM
When poor little Larry gets stuck in the ditch, Farmer George and Sidney
the horse come riding to his rescue through the snowstorm!
Paperback ISBN 1 84365 021 5 £4.99

FARMER GEORGE AND THE LOST CHICK
Farmer George's favourite hen, Clarrie, has lost one of her chicks. All the animals
in the farmyard join in the search, but they can't seem to find him anywhere!
Paperback ISBN 1 86205 432 0 £4.99

FARMER GEORGE AND THE FIELDMICE
It's harvest time on Farmer George's farm and a family of fieldmice realize that his
new combine harvester is heading for their home. Only Tam the dog can save them.
Paperback ISBN 1 86205 413 4 £4.99

FARMER GEORGE AND THE HEDGEHOGS
When Farmer George sets out to clear the yard of leaves, he discovers
that someone else has got there before him…
Paperback ISBN 1 86205 526 2 £4.99

FARMER GEORGE AND THE HUNGRY GUESTS
When food starts mysteriously disappearing from Farmer George's farm,
he and his dog, Tam, go in search of clues to discover the culprits.
Paperback ISBN 1 86205 531 9 £4.99

These books can be ordered direct from Pavilion Children's Books.
Please contact the Marketing Department. But try your bookshop first.